78   418

Date Due

Prince Lini

Signy

HALF A KINGDOM

AN ICELANDIC FOLKTALE

BY ANN McGOVERN

PICTURES BY NOLA LANGNER

FREDERICK WARNE

New York • London

HALF A KINGDOM is based on
an Icelandic folktale published in
the European folklore series *European Folk Tales,* Volume 1, a collec-
tion published under the auspices
of the Council For Cultural Co-
operation of the Council of Europe
by Rosenkilde and Bagger, Copen-
hagen, 1963.

Text Copyright © 1977 Ann McGovern
Illustrations Copyright © 1977 Nola Langner

Frederick Warne & Co., Inc.
New York, New York

First United Kingdom publication
Frederick Warne & Co., Ltd.,
London 1977

Manufactured in the United States of America
Library of Congress Catalog Card Number: 76-45305
ISBN: 0-7232-6137-7

1   2   3   4   5   6   7   8   9   10

FOR ANNIE C.

When you wake up in the morning,
you never can tell
what might happen to you during the day.

One fine morning,
Prince Lini woke up in his castle on the hill.
He didn't have the slightest idea what was going
to happen to him that day.

He rode into the forest with his friends.
Suddenly, from nowhere, a thick cold fog blew into the woods.
The cloud of fog covered the prince from head to toe.
A minute later the fog drifted away and was gone.
Gone, too, was Prince Lini.

His friends searched for him all that day
and all that night.
And in the morning they rode to the castle to tell the king
the strange story of the fog that rolled in from the sky
and took away his son.

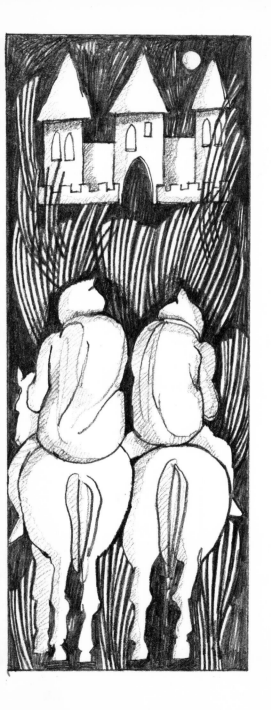

Now the king loved his son more than anything,
even more than the riches of his kingdom, which he loved very much.

He sent for his strongest men and his wisest men.
"Whoever finds Prince Lini," he said, "and brings him back to me,
will win half of my kingdom."

The strongest men (and those not so strong)
searched far and wide.
The wisest men (and those not so wise)
searched wide and far.
All over the kingdom people heard the news
that the prince had disappeared in a cloud of fog.

Anyone who had ever wanted half a kingdom set out
to search for the prince.
Because the king loved his riches so much,
most everyone in the kingdom was poor.
So most everyone took part in the search for the prince.

One fine morning,
Signy, a poor peasant girl, woke up in her cottage
at the edge of the forest.
She didn't have the slightest idea what was going
to happen to her that day.

But she had heard about the missing prince
and about the king's reward of half the kingdom.
She knew that the strongest and the wisest men had looked far and wide.
"I'll look near and narrow," she thought.

Signy knew the secret places of the forest better than anyone else.
She knew everything you had to know about living in the icy
winters of Iceland.
She knew how to walk against the wind.

She knew the best ways to keep warm.
And what to put on frost-bitten noses and toes
to make them feel better.

She put on a pair of sturdy shoes for walking
and took along some food.
And she set out to search for Prince Lini.

All that day she looked.
She saw nothing but tree shapes in the snow.
All that day she called.
She heard nothing but the song of the icy wind.

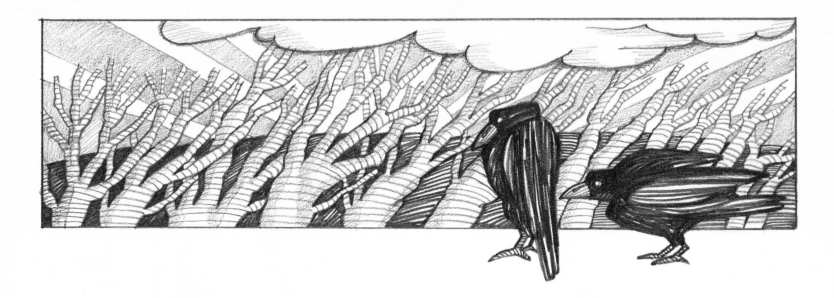

The sun began to set and the sky turned rosy.
Soon it would be dark.
Signy walked through a narrow place between the rocks
to her favorite warm cave and peered inside.
There, stretched out on a golden bed, was Prince Lini, fast asleep.
She ran into the cave and tried to wake him.
But he slept on, in a deep, deep sleep.

All of a sudden she heard a clattering, a chattering.
She ran to hide in the darkest corner of the cave.

Two troll girls—a tall troll and a shorter troll—entered the cave.
"Fee, Foo, Fum, Firl.
I smell the flesh of a human girl," sang the short troll.
"No," said the tall troll, "it's only Prince Lini."

Then the trolls whistled.
Signy listened carefully to the notes of the whistle.
Two swans flew into the cave.
The short troll said:

> *Sing O sing O swans of mine,*
> *Sing Prince Lini awake.*

The swans sang. Prince Lini stirred, rubbed his eyes and sat up.
"Now," said the short troll,
"for the ninety-seventh time, will you marry one of us?"
"Never," said the prince. "Never, never, never."
"You'll be sorry," the tall troll said.
Then she commanded the swans:

> Sing O sing O swans of mine,
> Sing Prince Lini asleep.

The swans sang and Prince Lini fell fast asleep again.
The swans flew out of the cave.

From her hiding place, Signy could see and hear everything.
The next morning the trolls left the cave
with a clattering and a chattering.
Signy crept from her hiding place.
She felt stiff and sore from crouching
the whole night in the dark corner.
She gave herself a shake all over.
Signy remembered how the trolls whistled,
and she whistled the same notes.
The swans flew into the cave. Signy said:

Sing O sing O swans of mine,
Sing Prince Lini awake.

The swans sang.

Prince Lini stirred, rubbed his eyes, sat up and rubbed his eyes again.

"Troll!" he said. "What has happened to you? You look very different."

"I'm not a troll," said Signy,

"and nothing has happened to me except that I found you. I'm Signy."

"I'm very pleased to meet you," said the prince.

The prince told Signy how the trolls had cast a spell upon him

with their magic fog and how they were holding him a prisoner

until he agreed to marry one of them.

Then Signy told the prince how sad the king was,
and how he had even offered half the kingdom to anyone
who found his son and brought him home.

"No one has found me yet except you," said the prince.
"But I don't know whether I *want* to be found.
It's nice and warm in this cave.
It's nice to have the trolls asking me to marry them every day."

Signy gave the prince a funny look.
"That wasn't true," said the prince.
"The real reason is that I don't want to go home.
It makes me sad to see how the kingdom is run.
And the king will listen to no one.
The rich are too rich and hardly work.
The poor are too poor and work too hard."

"Yes," said Signy sadly. "Everyone I know is poor
and we work all the time."
The prince looked at Signy and began to laugh.
He jumped up and down on the golden bed, laughing and laughing.

"What's so funny about being poor?" Signy asked.
"That's just it!" cried the prince.
"You won't be poor if you get half the kingdom and you can
share it with everyone!
Please, Signy, take me back to the king and take half the kingdom. Please!"

"First things first," said Signy.

"The first thing is to get you out of here."

"Why can't we run away right now while I'm awake?" said the prince.

"No," said Signy. "The trolls would surely send down their magic fog before we got out of the woods. They would make me a prisoner, too, along with you. You must find out from the trolls where they go and what they do during the day. It's the only way."

The prince agreed.

"Now let's play checkers," he said.

So they played checkers until the sun began to set and the sky turned rosy.

Then Signy whistled.

The swans flew into the cave and sang Prince Lini asleep.

Again Signy hid in the dark corner.

Soon the trolls came in with a clattering, a chattering.

They woke Prince Lini in their usual way.

And in their usual way they asked him their usual question.

"Now," said the tall troll, "for the ninety-eighth time,

will you marry one of us?"

The prince pretended to think about it.

"Tell me," he said, "where do you go and what do you do during the day?"

"We go to the big oak tree in the middle of the forest,"
the tall troll said.

"And we take out our giant golden egg," the short troll said.

"And we toss it back and forth, and back and forth,"
the tall troll said.

"What happens if you drop it?" Prince Lini asked.

"Oh, we never drop it," the short troll said.

"If we drop it and it breaks, we would disappear forever."

"Enough of this chatter," said the tall troll.

"Now for the ninety-ninth time,
will you marry one of us?"

"Never, never, never, never, NEVER!" said the prince.

"Oh," said the tall troll, shaking with rage,

"Tomorrow you will see how sorry you will be!"

"The end is near for you," said the short troll.

The trolls whistled. The swans sang and Prince Lini slept.

The next morning when the trolls left the cave,
Signy whistled for the swans.
The swans sang and Prince Lini awoke.
"You were wonderful," Signy said.
"Now we will go to the middle of the forest to the big oak tree.
You must do exactly what I tell you."
And she whispered her plan to the prince.

They left the cave and walked to the middle of the forest.
There they saw the two trolls under the big oak tree.
The trolls were throwing the giant golden egg to and fro, to and fro.

Signy whispered to the prince. "Be careful. Your life is in danger."
Prince Lini picked up a stone.
He aimed carefully and threw it.
The stone hit the giant golden egg. It fell to the ground,
broken to bits.

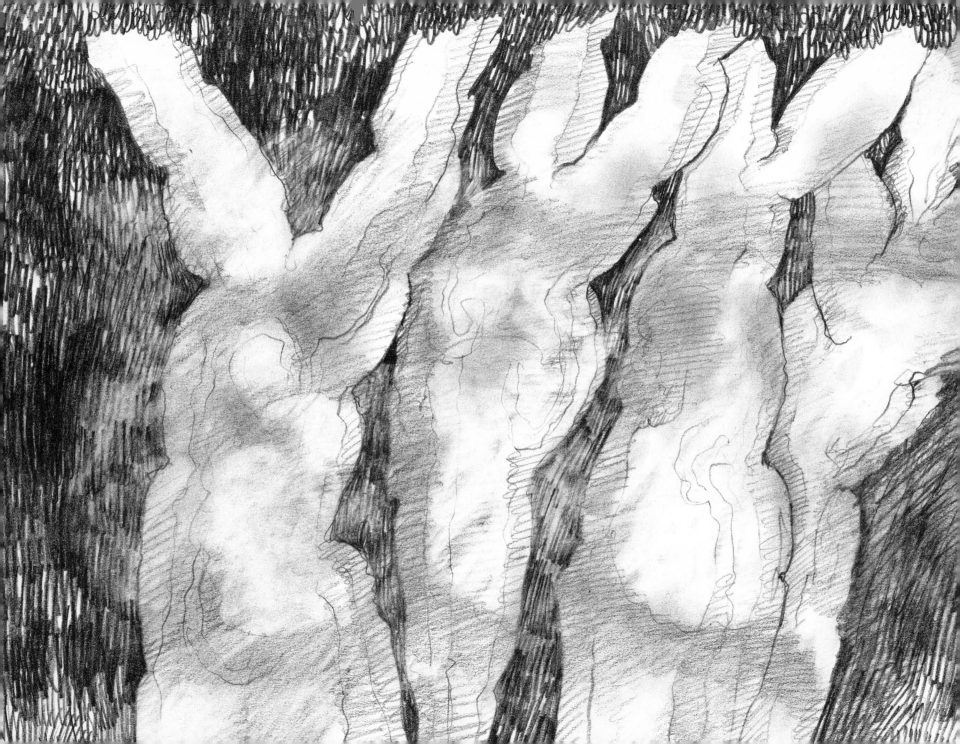

Suddenly from nowhere a thick cold fog blew into the woods.
The cloud of fog covered the two trolls.
A minute later the fog drifted away and was gone.
And gone, too, were the trolls.
Gone forever, to the place where trolls live.

Signy and Prince Lini ran all the way to the palace.
"Wait outside," Signy told the prince.
"It's better if I see your father alone."

"Who are you?" the king asked when he saw Signy, "And what do you want?"
"I am Signy, a peasant girl," she said,
"and I want half of your kingdom, for I found your son."
"Don't be silly," said the king. "How can a girl find my son when
my strongest and my wisest men could not find him!"
"That's too bad for them," Signy said. "If what I say is true,
will you keep your promise and give me half of your kingdom?"
"Go away," said the king. "It can't be true."

Signy ran to the door and flung it open.
The king was beside himself with joy to see his lost son.
After the two hugged and cried tears of happiness,
Prince Lini told his father about the trolls and the magic spell
and how Signy found him and freed him.

"Now will you give up half your kingdom?" Signy asked the king.

"Oh, my precious kingdom!" the king sighed.

"What about your precious son and your promise!" said the prince.

The king looked at Signy carefully.

"A girl like you found my son? A peasant girl—not even a princess!
But my precious son is right. And a promise is a promise.
I give you half my kingdom."

Prince Lini turned to Signy.
"I love you," he said. "Will you marry me?
I'll help you rule your half of the kingdom, if you like.
The poor won't have to work so hard or be so poor!"

"And the rich will have to work harder and they won't be so rich,"
the king mumbled.

Signy said, "Let's play checkers while I think it over."
They played checkers and Signy thought it over.
She thought it would be wonderful to marry Prince Lini.
"We can share half the kingdom and share adventures, too,
for the rest of our lives," she told him.
And that is exactly what they did, happily and forever after.

When you wake up in the morning—tomorrow morning—
you never can tell
what might happen to you during the day.

Prince Lini

Signy

3